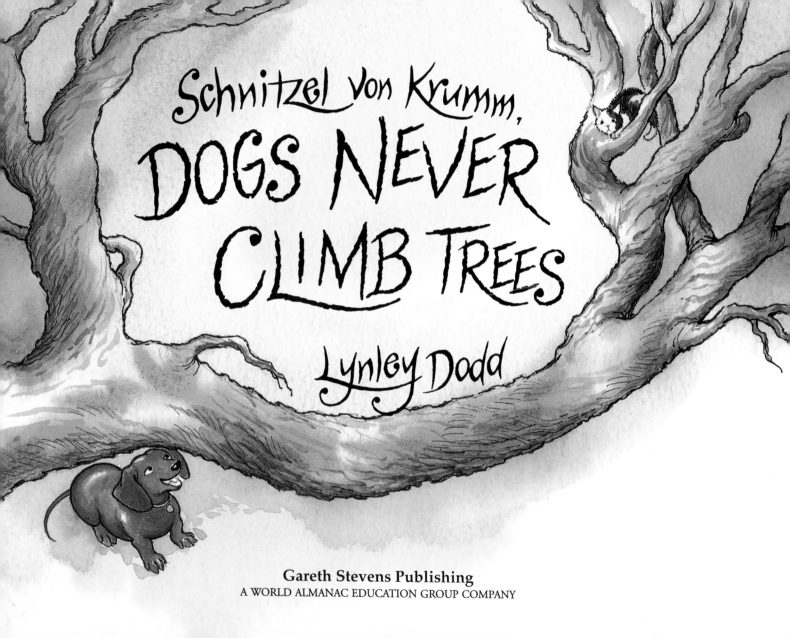

Schnitzel von Krumm, DOGS NEVER CLIMB TREES

Lynley Dodd

Gareth Stevens Publishing
A WORLD ALMANAC EDUCATION GROUP COMPANY

A dog to remember
is Schnitzel von Krumm,
with his very short legs
and his very low tum.
He can bury a bone
in a minute or two —
there are MANY
remarkable things
he can do.

He can hide in a woodpile
of branches and twigs,
and he disappears
into the holes
that he digs.

He fetches the paper,
his rug,
and his bowl.
Sometimes, his fetching
gets out of control.

He can hustle and tease
with the greatest of ease,
but everyone knows that
dogs
NEVER
climb
trees.

He can gallop and scamper
'round bushes and bends —
he has to run fast
to keep up with his friends.

He scatters the birds
when they're taking a bath
and sloshes the water
all over the path.

He can hustle and tease
with the greatest of ease,
but everyone knows that
dogs
NEVER
climb
trees.

He can ride on a skateboard.
He teeters on top
and flies through the air
when it comes to a
STOP.

His nose is so certain,
his sniffer so sound,
he can rustle a rabbit
from deep in the ground.

He can roll in the mud,
he can wallow and play
till he changes from brown
to a globulous gray.

He can hustle and tease
with the greatest of ease,
but everyone knows that
dogs
NEVER
climb
trees.

BUT
if they are bold
and adventurous, too . . .

it might just be possible . . .

maybe . . .

they DO!

31

Please visit our web site at: www.garethstevens.com
For a free color catalog describing Gareth Stevens Publishing's list of high-quality
books and multimedia programs, call 1-800-542-2595 (USA) or 1-800-387-3178 (Canada).
Gareth Stevens Publishing's fax: (414) 332-3567.

**Other GOLD STAR FIRST READER
Millennium Editions:**

A Dragon in a Wagon
Find Me a Tiger
Hairy Maclary from Donaldson's Dairy
Hairy Maclary Scattercat
Hairy Maclary, Sit
Hairy Maclary and Zachary Quack
Hairy Maclary's Bone
Hairy Maclary's Caterwaul Caper
Hairy Maclary's Rumpus at the Vet
Hairy Maclary's Showbusiness
Hedgehog Howdedo
Scarface Claw
Schnitzel von Krumm Forget-Me-Not
Schnitzel von Krumm's Basketwork

Slinky Malinki
Slinky Malinki, Open the Door
The Smallest Turtle
SNIFF-SNUFF-SNAP!
Wake Up, Bear

and also by Lynley Dodd:
The Minister's Cat ABC
Slinky Malinki Catflaps

Library of Congress Cataloging-in-Publication Data

Dodd, Lynley.
    Schnitzel von Krumm, dogs never climb trees / by Lynley Dodd.
        p. cm. — (Gold star first readers)
    Summary: Schnitzel von Krumm can do some remarkable things, but surely not climb a tree.
    ISBN 0-8368-4092-5 (lib. bdg.)
    [1. Dogs—Fiction. 2. Dachshunds—Fiction. 3. Stories in rhyme.] I. Title. II. Series.
    PZ8.3.D637Sai   2004
    [E]—dc22   2003059212

This edition first published in 2004 by
Gareth Stevens Publishing
A World Almanac Education Group Company
330 West Olive Street, Suite 100
Milwaukee, WI 53212 USA

First published in 2002 in New Zealand by Mallinson Rendel Publishers Ltd. Original © 2002 by Lynley Dodd.

Printed in the United States of America

1 2 3 4 5 6 7 8 9 08 07 06 05 04